# NAMES IN THE BLACK BOOK

## BY

## ROBERT E. HOWARD

**British Library Cataloguing-in-Publication Data**
A catalogue record for this book is available from the
British Library

# Robert E. Howard

Robert Ervin Howard was born in Peaster, Texas in 1906. During his youth, his family moved between a variety of Texan boomtowns, and Howard – a bookish and somewhat introverted child – was steeped in the violent myths and legends of the Old South. Although he loved reading and learning, Howard developed a distinctly Texan, hardboiled outlook on the world. He became a passionate fan of boxing, taking it up at an amateur level, and from the age of nine began to write adventure tales of semi-historical bloodshed. In 1919, when Howard was thirteen, his family moved to the Central Texas hamlet of Cross Plains, where he would stay for the rest of his life.

At fifteen Howard began to read the pulp magazines of the day, and to write more seriously. The December 1922 issue of his high school newspaper featured two of his stories, 'Golden Hope Christmas' and 'West is West'. In 1924 he sold his first piece – a short caveman tale titled 'Spear and Fang' – for $16 to the not-yet-famous *Weird Tales* magazine. He published with the magazine regularly over the next few years. 1929 was a breakout year for Howard, in that the 23-year-old writer began to sell to other magazines, such as *Ghost Stories* and *Argosy*, both of whom had previously sent him hundreds of rejection slips. In 1930, he began a correspondence with weird fiction master H. P. Lovecraft which ran up to his death six years later, and is regarded as one of the great correspondence cycles in all of fantasy literature.

It was partly due to Lovecraft's encouragement that Howard created his most famous character, Conan the Cimmerian. Conan – a barbarian-turned-King during the Hyborian Age, a mythical period of some 12,000 years ago – featured in seventeen *Weird Tales* stories between 1933 and 1936, and is now regarded as having spawned the 'sword and sorcery' genre, making Howard's influence on fantasy literature comparable to that of J. R. R. Tolkien's. The Conan stories have since been adapted many times, most famously in the series of films starring Arnold Schwarzenegger.

Howard was enjoying an all-time high in sales by the beginning of 1936, but he was also deeply upset by the ill health of his mother, who had fallen into a coma. On the morning of June 11, 1936, he asked an attending nurse whether she would ever recover, and the nurse replied negatively. Howard walked to his car, parked outside the family home in Cross Plains, and shot himself. He died eight hours later, aged just thirty.

"Three unsolved murders in a week are not so unusual--for River Street," grunted Steve Harrison, shifting his muscular bulk restlessly in his chair.

His companion lighted a cigarette and Harrison observed that her slim hand was none too steady. She was exotically beautiful, a dark, supple figure, with the rich colors of purple Eastern nights and crimson dawns in her dusky hair and red lips. But in her dark eyes Harrison glimpsed the shadow of fear. Only once before had he seen fear in those marvelous eyes, and the memory made him vaguely uneasy.

"It's your business to solve murders," she said.

"Give me a little time. You can't rush things, when you're dealing with the people of the Oriental quarter."

"You have less time than you think," she answered cryptically. "If you do not listen to me, you'll never solve these killings."

"I'm listening."

"But you won't believe. You'll say I'm hysterical--seeing ghosts and shying at shadows."

"Look here, Joan," he exclaimed impatiently. "Come to the point. You called me to your apartment and I came because you said you were in deadly danger. But now you're talking riddles about three men who were killed last week. Spill it plain, won't you?"

"Do you remember Erlik Khan?" she asked abruptly.

Involuntarily his hand sought his face, where a thin scar ran from temple to jaw-rim.

"I'm not likely to forget him," he said. "A Mongol who called himself Lord of the Dead. His idea was to combine all the Oriental criminal societies in America in one big organization, with himself at the head. He might have done it, too, if his own men hadn't turned on him."

"Erlik Khan has returned," she said.

"What!" His head jerked up and he glared at her incredulously. "What are you talking about? I saw him die, and so did you!"

"I saw his hood fall apart as Ali ibn Suleyman struck with his keen-edged scimitar," she answered. "I saw him roll to the floor and lie still. And then the house went up in flames, and the roof fell in, and only charred bones were ever found among the ashes. Nevertheless, Erlik Khan has returned."

Harrison did not reply, but sat waiting for further disclosures, sure they would come in an indirect way. Joan La Tour was half Oriental, and partook of many of the characteristics of her subtle kin.

"How did those three men die?" she asked, though he was aware that she knew as well as he.

"Li-crin, the Chinese merchant, fell from his own roof," he grunted. The people on the street heard him scream and then saw him come hurtling down. Might have been an accident--but middle-aged Chinese merchants don't go climbing around on roofs at midnight.

"Ibrahim ibn Achmet, the Syrian curio dealer, was bitten by a cobra. That might have been an accident too, only I know somebody dropped the snake on him through his skylight.

"Jacob Kossova, the Levantine exporter, was simply knifed in a back alley. Dirty jobs, all of them, and no apparent motive on the surface. But motives are hidden deep, in River Street. When I find the guilty parties I'll uncover the motives."

"And these murders suggest nothing to you?" exclaimed the girl, tense with suppressed excitement. "You do not see the link that connects them? You do not grasp the point they all have in common? Listen--all these men were formerly associated in one way or another with Erlik Khan!"

"Well?" he demanded. "That doesn't mean that the Khan's spook killed them! We found plenty of bones in the ashes of the house, but there were members of his gang in other parts of the city. His gigantic organization went to pieces, after his death, for lack of a leader, but the survivors were never uncovered. Some of them might be paying off old grudges."

"Then why did they wait so long to strike? It's been a year since we saw Erlik Khan die. I tell you, the Lord of the Dead himself, alive or dead, has returned and is striking down these men for one reason or another. Perhaps they refuse to do his bidding once more. Five were marked for death. Three have fallen."

"How do you know that?" said he.

"Look!" From beneath the cushions of the divan on which she sat she drew something, and rising, came and bent beside him while she unfolded it.

It was a square piece of parchment-like substance, black and glossy. On it were written five names, one below the other, in a bold flowing hand--and in crimson, like spilled blood. Through the first three names a crimson bar had been drawn. They were the names of Li-chin, Ibrahim ibn Achmet, and Jacob Kossova. Harrison grunted explosively. The last two names, as yet unmarred, were those of Joan La Tour and Stephen Harrison.

"Where did you get this?" he demanded.

"It was shoved under my door last night, while I slept. If all the doors and windows had not been locked, the police would have found it pinned to my corpse this morning."

"But still I don't see what connection--"

"It is a page from the Black Book of Erlik Khan!" she cried. "The book of the dead! I have seen it, when I was a subject of his in the old days. There he kept accounts of his enemies, alive and dead. I saw that book, open, the very day of the night Ali ibn Suleyman killed him--a big book with jade-hinged ebony covers and glossy black parchment

6

pages. Those names were not in it then; they have been written in since Erlik Khan died--and that is Erlik Khan's handwriting!"

If Harrison was impressed he failed to show it.

"Does he keep his books in English?"

"No, in a Mongolian script. This is for our benefit. And I know we are hopelessly doomed. Erlik Khan never warned his victims unless he was sure of them."

"Might be a forgery," grunted the detective.

"No! No man could imitate Erlik Khan's hand. He wrote those names himself. He has come back from the dead! Hell could not hold a devil as black as he!" Joan was losing some of her poise in her fear and excitement. She ground out the half-consumed cigarette and broke the cover of a fresh carton. She drew forth a slim white cylinder and tossed the package on the table. Harrison took it up and absently extracted one for himself.

"Our names are in the Black Book! It is a sentence of death from which there is no appeal!" She struck a match and was lifting it, when Harrison struck the cigarette from her with a startled oath. She fell back on the divan, bewildered at the violence of his action, and he caught up the package and began gingerly to remove the contents.

"Where'd you get these things?"

"Why, down at the corner drug store, I guess," she stammered. "That's where I usually--"

"Not these you didn't," he grunted. "These fags have been specially treated. I don't know what it is, but I've seen one puff of the stuff knock a man stone dead. Some kind of a hellish Oriental drug mixed with the tobacco. You were out of your apartment while you were phoning me--"

"I was afraid my wire was tapped," she answered. "I went to a public booth down the street."

"And it's my guess somebody entered your apartment while you were gone and switched cigarettes on you. I only got a faint whiff of the stuff when I started to put that fag in my mouth, but it's unmistakable. Smell it yourself. Don't be afraid. It's deadly only when ignited."

She obeyed, and turned pale.

"I told you! We were the direct cause of Erlik Khan's overthrow! If you hadn't smelt that drug, we'd both be dead now, as he intended!"

"Well," he grunted, "it's a cinch somebody's after you, anyway. I still say it can't be Erlik Khan, because nobody could live after the lick on the head I saw Ali ibn Suleyman hand him, and I don't believe in ghosts. But you've got to be protected until I run down whoever is being so free with his poisoned cigarettes."

"What about yourself? Your name's in his book, too."

"Never mind me," Harrison growled pugnaciously. "I reckon I can take care of myself." He looked capable enough, with his cold blue eyes, and the muscles bulging in his coat. He had shoulders like a bull.

"This wing's practically isolated from the rest of the building," he said, "and you've got the third floor to yourself?"

"Not only the third floor of the wing," she answered. "There's no one else on the third floor anywhere in the building at present."

"That makes it fine!" he exclaimed irritably. "Somebody could sneak in and cut your throat without disturbing anyone. That's what they'll try, too, when they realize the cigarettes didn't finish you. You'd better move to a hotel."

"That wouldn't make any difference," she answered, trembling. Her nerves obviously were in a bad way. "Erlik Khan would find me, anywhere. In a hotel, with people coming and going all the time, and the rotten locks they have on the doors, with transoms and fire escapes and everything, it would just be that much easier for him."

"Well, then, I'll plant a bunch of cops around here."

"That wouldn't do any good, either. Erlik Khan has killed again and again in spite of the police. They do not understand his ways."

"That's right," he muttered uncomfortably aware of a conviction that to summon men from headquarters would surely be signing those men's death warrants, without accomplishing anything else. It was absurd to suppose that the dead Mongol fiend was behind these murderous attacks, yet--Harrison's flesh crawled along his spine at the memory of things that had taken place in River Street--things he had never reported, because he did not wish to be thought either a liar or a madman. The dead do not return--but what seems absurd on Thirty-ninth Boulevard takes on a different aspect among the haunted labyrinths of the Oriental quarter.

"Stay with me!" Joan's eyes were dilated, and she caught Harrison's arm with hands that shook violently. "We can defend these rooms! While one sleeps the other can watch! Do not call the police; their blunders would doom us. You have worked in the quarter for years, and are worth more than the whole police force. The mysterious instincts that are a part of my Eastern heritage are alert to danger. I feel peril for us both, near, creeping closer, gliding around us like serpents in the darkness!"

"But I can't stay here," he scowled worriedly. "We can't barricade ourselves and wait for them to starve us out. I've got to hit back--find out who's behind all this. The best defense is a good offense. But I can't leave you here unguarded, either. Damn!" He clenched his big fists and shook his head like a baffled bull in his perplexity.

"There is one man in the city besides yourself I could trust," she said suddenly. "One worth more than all the police. With him guarding me I could sleep safely."

"Who is he?"

"Khoda Khan."

"That fellow? Why, I thought he'd skipped months ago."

"No; he's been hiding in Levant Street."

"But he's a confounded killer himself!"

"No, he isn't; not according to his standards, which means as much to him as yours do to you. He's an Afghan who was raised in a code of blood-feud and vengeance. He's as honorable according to his creed of life as you or I. And he's my friend. He'd die for me."

"I reckon that means you've been hiding him from the law," said Harrison with a searching glance which she did not seek to evade. He made no further comment. River Street is not South Park Avenue. Harrison's own methods were not always orthodox, but they generally got results.

"Can you reach him?" he asked abruptly. She nodded.

"Alright. Call him and tell him to beat it up here. Tell him he won't be molested by the police, and after the brawl's over, he can go back into hiding. But after that it's open season if I catch him. Use your phone. Wire may be tapped, but we'll have to take the chance. I'll go downstairs and use the booth in the office. Lock the door, and don't open it to anybody until I get back."

When the bolts clicked behind him, Harrison turned down the corridor toward the stairs. The apartment house boasted no elevator. He watched all sides warily as he went.

11

A peculiarity of architecture had, indeed, practically isolated that wing. The wall opposite Joan's doors was blank. The only way to reach the other suites on that floor was to descend the stair and ascend another on the other side of the building.

As he reached the stair he swore softly; his heel had crunched a small vial on the first step. With some vague suspicion of a planted poison trap he stooped and gingerly investigated the splintered bits and the spilled contents. There was a small pool of colorless liquid which gave off a pungent, musky odor, but there seemed nothing lethal about it.

"Some damned Oriental perfume Joan dropped, I reckon," he decided. He descended the twisting stair without further delay and was presently in the booth in the office which opened on the street; a sleepy clerk dozed behind the desk.

Harrison got the chief of police on the wire and began abruptly.

"Say, Hoolihan, you remember that Afghan, Khoda Khan, who knifed a Chinaman about three months ago? Yes, that's the one. Well, listen: I'm using him on a job for a while, so tell your men to lay off, if they see him. Pass the word along pronto. Yes, I know it's very irregular; so's the job I hold down. In this case it's the choice of using a fugitive from the law, or seeing a law-abiding citizen murdered.

Never mind what it's all about. This is my job, and I've got to handle it my own way. All right; thanks."

He hung up the receiver, thought vigorously for a few minutes, and then dialed another number that was definitely not related to the police station. In place of the chief's booming voice there sounded at the other end of the wire a squeaky whine framed in the argot of the underworld.

"Listen, Johnny," said Harrison with his customary abruptness, "you told me you thought you had a lead on the Kossova murder. What about it?"

"It wasn't no lie, boss!" The voice at the other end trembled with excitement. "I got a tip, and it's big!--big! I can't spill it over the phone, and I don't dare stir out. But if you'll meet me at Shan Yang's hop joint, I'll give you the dope. It'll knock you loose from your props, believe me it will!"

"I'll be there in an hour," promised the detective. He left the booth and glanced briefly out into the street. It was a misty night, as so many River Street nights are. Traffic was only a dim echo from some distant, busier section. Drifting fog dimmed the street lamps, shrouding the forms of occasional passers-by. The stage was set for murder; it only awaited the appearance of the actors in the dark drama.

Harrison mounted the stairs again. They wound up out of the office and up into the third story wing without opening upon the second floor at all. The architecture, like much of it in or near the Oriental section, was rather unusual. People of the quarter were notoriously fond of privacy, and even apartment houses were built with this passion in mind. His feet made no sound on the thickly carpeted stairs, though a slight crunching at the top step reminded him of the broken vial again momentarily. He had stepped on the splinters.

He knocked at the locked door, answered Joan's tense challenge and was admitted. He found the girl more self-possessed.

"I talked with Khoda Khan. He's on his way here now. I warned him that the wire might be tapped--that our enemies might know as soon as I called him, and try to stop him on his way here."

"Good," grunted the detective. "While I'm waiting for him I'll have a look at your suite."

There were four rooms, drawing room in front, with a large bedroom behind it, and behind that two smaller rooms, the maid's bedroom and the bathroom. The maid was not there, because Joan had sent her away at the first intimation of danger threatening. The corridor ran parallel with the suite, and the drawing room, large bedroom and bathroom opened upon it. That made three doors to consider. The drawing room had one big east window, overlooking the street, and one on the south. The big bedroom had one south window, and the maid's room one south and one west window. The bathroom had one window, a small one in the west wall, overlooking a small court bounded by a tangle of alleys and board-fenced backyards.

"Three outside doors and six windows to be watched, and this the top story," muttered the detective. "I still think I ought to get some cops here." But he spoke without conviction. He was investigating the bathroom when Joan called him cautiously from the drawing room, telling him that she thought she had heard a faint scratching outside the door. Gun in hand he opened the bathroom door and peered out into the corridor. It was empty. No shape of horror stood before the drawing room door. He closed the door, called reassuringly to the girl, and completed his inspection, grunting approval. Joan La Tour was a daughter of the Oriental quarter. Long ago she had provided against secret enemies as far as special locks and bolts could provide. The windows were guarded with heavy iron-braced shutters, and there was no trapdoor, dumb waiter nor skylight anywhere in the suite.

"Looks like you're ready for a siege," he commented.

"I am. I have canned goods laid away to last for weeks. With Khoda Khan I can hold the fort indefinitely. If things get too hot for you, you'd better come back here yourself--if you can. It's safer than the police station--unless they burn the house down."

A soft rap on the door brought them both around.

"Who is it?" called Joan warily.

"I, Khoda Khan, sahiba," came the answer in a low-pitched, but strong and resonant voice. Joan sighed deeply and unlocked the door. A tall figure bowed with a stately gesture and entered.

Khoda Khan was taller than Harrison, and though he lacked something of the American's sheer bulk, his shoulders were equally broad, and his garments could not conceal the hard lines of his limbs, the tigerish suppleness of his motions. His garb was a curious combination of costume, which is common in River Street. He wore a turban which well set off his hawk nose and black beard, and a long silk coat hung nearly to his knees. His trousers were conventional, but a silk sash girdled his lean waist, and his foot-gear was Turkish slippers.

In any costume it would have been equally evident that there was something wild and untamable about the man. His eyes blazed as no civilized man's ever did, and his sinews were like coiled springs under his coat. Harrison felt much as he would have felt if a panther had padded into the room, for the moment placid but ready at an instant's notice to go flying into flaming-eyed, red-taloned action.

"I thought you'd left the country," he said.

The Afghan smiled, a glimmer of white amidst the dark tangle of his beard.

"Nay, sahib. That son of a dog I knifed did not die."

"You're lucky he didn't," commented Harrison. "If you kill him you'll hang, sure."

"Inshallah," agreed Khoda Khan cheerfully. "But it was a matter of izzat--honor. The dog fed me swine's flesh. But no matter. The memsahib called me and I came."

"Alright. As long as she needs your protection the police won't arrest you. But when the matter's finished, things stand as they were. I'll give you time to hide again, if you wish, and then I'll try to catch you as I have in the past. Or if you want to surrender and stand trial, I'll promise you as much leniency as possible."

"You speak fairly," answered Khoda Khan. "I will protect the memsahib, and when our enemies are dead, you and I will begin our feud anew."

"Do you know anything about these murders?"

"Nay, sahib. The memsahib called me, saying Mongol dogs threatened her. I came swiftly, over the roofs, lest they seek to ambush me. None molested me. But here is something I found outside the door."

He opened his hand and exhibited a bit of silk, evidently torn from his sash. On it lay a crushed object that Harrison did not recognize. But Joan recoiled with a low cry.

"God! A black scorpion of Assam!"

"Aye--whose sting is death. I saw it running up and down before the door, seeking entrance. Another man might have stepped upon it without seeing it, but I was on my

17

guard, for I smelled the Flower of Death as I came up the stairs. I saw the thing at the door and crushed it before it could sting me."

"What do you mean by the Flower of Death?" demanded Harrison.

"It grows in the jungles where these vermin abide. Its scent attracts them as wine draws a drunkard. A trail of the juice had somehow been laid to this door. Had the door been opened before I slew it, it would have darted in and struck whoever happened to be in its way."

Harrison swore under his breath, remembering the faint scratching noise Joan had heard outside the door.

"I get it now! They put a bottle of that juice on the stairs where it was sure to be stepped on. I did step on it, and broke it, and got the liquid on my shoe. Then I tracked down the stairs, leaving the scent wherever I stepped. Came back upstairs, stepped in the stuff again and tracked it on through the door. Then somebody downstairs turned that scorpion loose--the devil!! That means they've been in this house since I was downstairs!--may be hiding somewhere here now! But somebody had to come into the office to put the scorpion on the trail--I'll ask the clerk--"

"He sleeps like the dead," said Khoda Khan. "He did not waken when I entered and mounted the stairs. What matters if the house is full of Mongols? These doors are strong, and I am alert!" From beneath his coat he drew the terrible Khyber knife--a yard long, with an edge like a razor. "I have slain men with this," he announced, grinning like a bearded mountain devil. "Pathans, Indians, a Russian or so. These Mongols are dogs on whom the good steel will be shamed."

"Well," grunted Harrison. "I've got an appointment that's overdue now. I feel queer walking out and leaving you two to fight these devils alone. But there'll be no safety for us until I've smashed this gang at its root, and that's what I'm out to do."

"They'll kill you as you leave the building," said Joan with conviction.

"Well, I've got to risk it. If you're attacked call the police anyway, and call me, at Shan Yang's joint. I'll come back here some time before dawn. But I'm hoping the tip I expect to get will enable me to hit straight at whoever's after us."

He went down the hallway with an eerie feeling of being watched and scanned the stairs as if he expected to see it swarming with black scorpions, and he shied wide of the broken glass on the step. He had an uncomfortable sensation of duty ignored, in spite of himself, though he knew that his two companions did not want the police, and that in dealing with the East it is better to heed the advice of the East.

The clerk still sagged behind his desk. Harrison shook him without avail. The man was not asleep; he was drugged. But his heartbeat was regular, and the detective believed he was in no danger. Anyway, Harrison had no more time to waste. If he kept Johnny Kleck waiting too long, the fellow might become panicky and bolt, to hide in some rat-run for weeks.

He went into the street, where the lamps gleamed luridly through the drifting river mist, half expecting a knife to be thrown at him, or to find a cobra coiled on the seat of his automobile. But he found nothing his suspicion anticipated, even though he lifted the hood and the rumble-seat to see if a bomb had been planted. Satisfying himself at last, he climbed in and the girl watching him through the slits of a third-story shutter sighed relievedly to see him roar away unmolested.

Khoda Khan had gone through the rooms, giving approval in his beard of the locks, and having extinguished the lights in the other chambers he returned to the drawing room, where he turned out all lights there except one small desk lamp. It shed a pool of light in the center of the room, leaving the rest in shadowy vagueness.

"Darkness baffles rogues as well as honest men," he said sagely, "and I see like a cat in the dark."

He sat cross-legged near the door that let into the bedroom, which he left partly open. He merged with the shadows so that all of him Joan could make out with any distinctness was his turban and the glimmer of his eyes as he turned his head.

"We will remain in this room, sahiba," he said. "Having failed with poison and reptile, it is certain that men will next be sent. Lie down on that divan and sleep, if you can. I will keep watch."

Joan obeyed, but she did not sleep. Her nerves seemed to thrum with tautness. The silence of the house oppressed her, and the few noises of the street made her start.

Khoda Khan sat motionless as a statue, imbued with the savage patience and immobility of the hills that bred him. Grown to manhood on the raw barbaric edge of the world, where survival depended on personal ability, his senses were whetted keener than is possible for civilized men. Even Harrison's trained faculties were blunt in comparison. Khoda Khan could still smell the faint aroma of the Flower of Death, mingled with the acrid odor of the crushed scorpion. He heard and identified every sound in or outside the house--knew which were natural, and which were not.

He heard the sounds on the roof long before his warning hiss brought Joan upright on the divan. The Afghan's eyes glowed like phosphorus in the shadows and his teeth glimmered dimly in a savage grin. Joan looked at him inquiringly. Her civilized ears heard nothing. But he heard and with his ears followed the sounds accurately and located the place where they halted. Joan heard something then, a faint scratching somewhere in the building, but she did not identify it--as Khoda Khan did--as the forcing of the shutters on the bathroom window.

With a quick reassuring gesture to her, Khoda Khan rose and melted like a slinking leopard into the darkness of the bedroom. She took up a blunt-nosed automatic, with no great conviction of reliance upon it, and groped on the table for a bottle of wine, feeling an intense need of stimulants. She was shaking in every limb and cold sweat was gathering on her flesh. She remembered the cigarettes, but the unbroken seal on the bottle reassured her. Even the wisest have their thoughtless moments. It was not until she had begun to drink that the peculiar flavor made her realize that the man who had shifted the cigarettes might just as easily have taken a bottle of wine and left another in its place, a facsimile that included an unbroken seal. She fell back on the divan, gagging.

Khoda Khan wasted no time, because he heard other sounds, out in the hall. His ears told him, as he crouched by the bathroom door, that the shutters had been forced-- done almost in silence, a job that a white man would have made sound like an explosion in an iron foundry--and now the window was being jimmied. Then he heard something stealthy and bulky drop into the room. Then it was that he threw open the door and charged in like a typhoon, his long knife held low.

Enough light filtered into the room from outside to limn a powerful, crouching figure, with dim snarling yellow features. The intruder yelped explosively, started a motion--and then the long Khyber knife, driven by an arm nerved to the fury of the Himalayas, ripped him open from groin to breastbone.

Khoda Khan did not pause. He knew there was only one man in the room, but through the open window he saw a thick rope dangling from above. He sprang forward, grasped it with both hands and heaved backward like a bull. The men on the roof holding it released it to keep from being jerked headlong over the edge, and he tumbled backward, sprawling over the corpse, the loose rope in his hands. He yelped exultantly, then sprang up and glided to the door that opened into the corridor. Unless they had another rope, which was unlikely, the men on the roof were temporarily out of the fight.

He flung open the door and ducked deeply. A hatchet cut a great chip out the jamb, and he stabbed upward once, then sprang over a writhing body into the corridor, jerking a big pistol from its hidden scabbard.

The bright light of the corridor did not blind him. He saw a second hatchet-man crouching by the bedroom door, and a man in the silk robes of a mandarin working at the lock of the drawing room door. He was between them and the stairs. As they wheeled toward him he shot the hatchet-man in the belly. An automatic spat in the hand of the mandarin, and Khoda Khan felt the wind of the bullet. The next instant his own gun roared again and the Manchu staggered, the pistol flying from a hand that was suddenly a dripping red pulp. Then he whipped a long knife from his robes with his left hand and came along the corridor like a hurricane, his eyes glaring and his silk garments whipping about him.

Khoda Khan shot him through the head and the mandarin fell so near his feet that the long knife stuck into the floor and quivered a matter of inches from the Afghan's slipper.

But Khoda Khan paused only long enough to pass his knife through the hatchet-man he had shot in the belly--for his fighting ethics were those of the savage Hills--and then he turned and ran back into the bathroom. He fired a shot through the window, though the men on the roof were making further demonstration, and then ran through the bedroom, snapping on lights as he went.

"I have slain the dogs, sahiba!" he exclaimed. "By Allah, they have tasted lead and steel! Others are on the roof but they are helpless for the moment. But men will come to investigate the shots, that being the custom of the sahibs, so it is expedient that we decide on our further actions, and the proper lies to tell--Allah!"

Joan La Tour stood bolt upright, clutching the back of the divan. Her face was the color of marble, and the expression was rigid too, like a mask of horror carved in stone. Her dilated eyes blazed like weird black fire.

"Allah shield us against Shaitan the Damned!" ejaculated Khoda Khan, making a sign with his fingers that antedated Islam by some thousands of years. "What has happened to you, sahiba?"

He moved toward her, to be met by a scream that sent him cowering back, cold sweat starting out on his flesh.

"Keep back!" she cried in a voice he did not recognize. "You are a demon! You are all demons! I see you! I hear your cloven feet padding in the night! I see your eyes blazing from the shadows! Keep your taloned hands from me! Aie!" Foam flecked her lips as she screamed blasphemies in English and Arabic that made Khoda Khan's hair stand stiffly on end.

"Sahiba!" he begged, trembling like a leaf. "I am no demon! I am Khoda Khan! I--" His outstretched hand touched her, and with an awful shriek she turned and darted for the door, tearing at the bolts. He sprang to stop her, but in her frenzy she was even quicker than he. She whipped the door open, eluded his grasping hand and flew down the corridor, deaf to his anguished yells.

When Harrison left Joan's house, he drove straight to Shan Yang's dive, which, in the heart of River Street, masqueraded as a low-grade drinking joint. It was late. Only a few derelicts huddled about the bar, and he noticed that the barman was a Chinaman that he had never seen before. He stared impassively at Harrison, but jerked a thumb toward the back door, masked by dingy curtains, when the detective asked abruptly: "Johnny Kleck here?"

Harrison passed through the door, traversed a short dimly-lighted hallway and rapped authoritatively on the door at the other end. In the silence he heard rats scampering. A steel disk in the center of the door shifted and a slanted black eye glittered in the opening.

"Open the door, Shan Yang," ordered Harrison impatiently, and the eye was withdrawn, accompanied by the rattling of bolts and chains.

He pushed open the door and entered the room whose illumination was scarcely better than that of the corridor. It was a large, dingy, drab affair, lined with bunks. Fires sputtered in braziers, and Shan Yang was making his way to his accustomed seat behind a low counter near the wall. Harrison spent but a single casual glance on the familiar figure, the well-known dingy silk jacket worked in gilt dragons. Then he strode across the room to a door in the wall opposite the counter to which Shan Yang was making his way. This was an opium joint and Harrison knew it--knew those figures in the bunks were Chinamen sleeping the sleep of the smoke. Why he had not raided it, as he had raided and destroyed other opium-dens, only Harrison could have said. But law-enforcement on River Street is not the orthodox routine it is on Baskerville Avenue, for instance. Harrison's reasons were those of expediency and necessity. Sometimes certain conventions have to be sacrificed for the sake of more important gains--especially when the law-enforcement of a whole district (and in the Oriental quarter) rests on one's shoulders.

A characteristic smell pervaded the dense atmosphere, in spite of the reek of dope and unwashed bodies--the dank odor of the river, which hangs over the River Street dives or wells up from their floors like the black intangible spirit of the quarter itself. Shan Yang's dive, like many others, was built on the very bank of the river. The back room projected out over the water on rotting piles, at which the black river lapped hungrily.

Harrison opened the door, entered and pushed it to behind him, his lips framing a greeting that was never uttered. He stood dumbly, glaring.

He was in a small dingy room, bare except for a crude table and some chairs. An oil lamp on the table cast a smoky light. And in that light he saw Johnny Kleck. The man stood bolt upright against the far wall, his arms spread like a crucifix, rigid, his eyes glassy and staring, his mean, ratty features twisted in a frozen grin. He did not speak, and Harrison's gaze, traveling down him, halted with a shock. Johnny's feet did not touch the floor by several inches--

Harrison's big blue pistol jumped into his hand. Johnny Kleck was dead, that grin was a contortion of horror and agony. He was crucified to the wall by skewer-like dagger blades through his wrists and ankles, his ears spiked to the wall to keep his head upright. But that was not what had killed him. The bosom of Johnny's shirt was charred, and there was a round, blackened hole.

Feeling suddenly sick the detective wheeled, opened the door and stepped back into the larger room. The light seemed dimmer, the smoke thicker than ever. No mumblings came from the bunks; the fires in the braziers burned blue, with weird sputterings. Shan Yang crouched behind the counter. His shoulders moved as if he were tallying beads on an abacus.

"Shan Yang!" the detective's voice grated harshly in the murky silence. "Who's been in that room tonight besides Johnny Kleck?"

The man behind the counter straightened and looked full at him, and Harrison felt his skin crawl. Above the gilt-worked jacket an unfamiliar face returned his gaze. That was no Shan Yang; it was a man he had never seen--it was a Mongol. He started and stared about him as the men in the bunks rose with supple ease. They were not Chinese; they were Mongols to a man, and their slanted black eyes were not clouded by drugs.

With a curse Harrison sprang toward the outer door and with a rush they were on him. His gun crashed and a man staggered in mid-stride. Then the lights went out, the braziers were overturned, and in the stygian blackness hard bodies caromed against the detective. Long-nailed fingers clawed at his throat, thick arms locked about his waist and legs. Somewhere a sibilant voice was hissing orders.

Harrison's mauling left worked like a piston, crushing flesh and bone; his right wielded the gun barrel like a club. He forged toward the unseen door blindly, dragging his assailants by sheer strength. He seemed to be wading through a solid mass, as if the darkness had turned to bone and muscle about him. A knife licked through his coat, stinging his skin, and then he gasped as a silk cord looped about his neck, shutting off his wind, sinking deeper and deeper into the straining flesh. Blindly he jammed the muzzle against the nearest body and pulled the trigger. At the muffled concussion something fell away from him and the strangling agony lessened. Gasping for breath he groped and tore the cord away--then he was borne down under a rush of heavy bodies and something smashed savagely against his head. The darkness exploded in a shower of sparks that were instantly quenched in stygian blackness.

   \* \* \*

The smell of the river was in Steve Harrison's nostrils as he regained his addled senses, river-scent mingled with the odor of stale blood. The blood, he realized, when he had enough sense to realize anything, was clotted on his own scalp. His head swam and he tried to raise a hand to it, thereby discovering that he was bound hand and foot with cords that cut into the flesh. A candle was dazzling his eyes, and for awhile he could see nothing else. Then things began to assume their proper proportions, and objects grew out of nothing and became identifiable.

He was lying on a bare floor of new, unpainted wood, in a large square chamber, the walls of which were of stone, without paint or plaster. The ceiling was likewise of stone, with heavy, bare beams, and there was an open trap door almost directly above him, through which, in spite of the candle, he got a glimpse of stars. Fresh air flowed through that trap, bearing with it the river-smell stronger than ever. The chamber was bare of furniture, the candle stuck in a niche in the wall. Harrison swore, wondering if he was delirious. This was like an experience in a dream, with everything unreal and distorted.

He tried to struggle to a sitting position, but that made his head swim, so that he lay back and swore fervently. He yelled wrathfully, and a face peered down at him through the trap--a square, yellow face with beady slanted eyes. He cursed the face and it mocked him and was withdrawn. The noise of the door softly opening checked Harrison's profanity and he wriggled around to glare at the intruder.

And he glared in silence, feeling an icy prickling up and down his spine. Once before he had lain bound and helpless, staring up at a tall black-robed figure whose yellow eyes glimmered from the shadow of a dusky hood. But that man was dead; Harrison had seen him cut down by the scimitar of a maddened Druse.

"Erlik Khan!" The words were forced out of him. He licked lips suddenly dry.

"Aie!" It was the same ghostly, hollow voice that had chilled him in the old days. "Erlik Khan, the Lord of the Dead."

"Are you a man or a ghost?" demanded Harrison.

"I live."

"But I saw Ali ibn Suleyman kill you!" exclaimed the detective. "He slashed you across the head with a heavy sword that was sharp as a razor. He was a stronger man than I am. He struck with the full power of his arm. Your hood fell in two pieces--"

"And I fell like a dead man in my own blood," finished Erlik Khan. "But the steel cap I wore--as I wear now--under my hood, saved my life as it has more than once. The terrible stroke cracked it across the top and cut my scalp, fracturing my skull and causing concussion of the brain. But I lived, and some of my faithful followers, who escaped the sword of the Druse, carried me down through the subterranean tunnels which led from my house, and so I escaped the burning building. But I lay like a dead man for weeks, and it was not until a very wise man was brought from Mongolia that I recovered my senses, and sanity.

"But now I am ready to take up my work where I left off, though I must rebuild much. Many of my former followers had forgotten my authority. Some required to be taught anew who was master."

"And you've been teaching them," grunted Harrison, recovering his pugnacious composure.

"True. Some examples had to be made. One man fell from a roof, a snake bit another, yet another ran into knives in a dark alley. Then there was another matter. Joan La Tour betrayed me in the old days. She knows too many secrets. She had to die. So that she might taste agony in anticipation, I sent her a page from my book of the dead."

"Your devils killed Kleck," accused Harrison.

"Of course. All wires leading from the girl's apartment house are tapped. I myself heard your conversation with Kleck. That is why you were not attacked when you left the building. I saw that you were playing into my hands. I sent my men to take possession of Shan Yang's dive. He had no more use for his jacket, presently, so one donned it to deceive you. Kleck had somehow learned of my return; these stool pigeons are clever. But he had time to regret. A man dies hard with a white-hot point of iron bored through his breast."

Harrison said nothing and presently the Mongol continued.

"I wrote your name in my book because I recognized you as my most dangerous opponent. It was because of you that Ali ibn Suleyman turned against me.

"I am rebuilding my empire again, but more solidly. First I shall consolidate River Street, and create a political machine to rule the city. The men in office now do not suspect my existence. If all were to die, it would not be hard to find others to fill their places--men who are not indifferent to the clink of gold."

"You're mad," growled Harrison. "Control a whole city government from a dive in River Street?"

"It has been done," answered the Mongol tranquilly. "I will strike like a cobra from the dark. Only the men who obey my agent will live. He will be a white man, a figurehead whom men will think the real power, while I remain unseen. You might have been he, if you had a little more intelligence."

He took a bulky object from under his arm, a thick book with glossy black covers--ebony with green jade hinges. He riffled the night-hued pages and Harrison saw they were covered with crimson characters.

"My book of the dead," said Erlik Khan. "Many names have been crossed out. Many more have been added since I recovered my sanity. Some of them would interest you; they include names of the mayor, the chief of police, district attorney, a number of aldermen."

"That lick must have addled your brains permanently," snarled Harrison. "Do you think you can substitute a whole city government and get away with it?"

"I can and will. These men will die in various ways, and men of my own choice will succeed them in office. Within a year I will hold this city in the palm of my hand, and there will be none to interfere with me."

Lying staring up at the bizarre figure, whose features were, as always, shadowed beyond recognition by the hood, Harrison's flesh crawled with the conviction that the Mongol was indeed mad. His crimson dreams, always ghastly, were too grotesque and incredible for the visions of a wholly sane man. Yet he was dangerous as a maddened cobra. His monstrous plot must ultimately fail, yet he held the lives of many men in his hand. And Harrison, on whom the city relied for protection from whatever menace the Oriental quarter might spawn, lay bound and helpless before him. The detective cursed in fury.

"Always the man of violence," mocked Erlik Khan, with the suggestion of scorn in his voice. "Barbarian! Who lays his trust in guns and blades, who would check the stride of imperial power with blows of the naked fists! Brainless arm striking blind blows! Well, you have struck your last. Smell the river damp that creeps in through the ceiling? Soon it shall enfold you utterly and your dreams and aspirations will be one with the mist of the river."

"Where are we?" demanded Harrison.

"On an island below the city, where the marshes begin. Once there were warehouses here, and a factory, but they were abandoned as the city grew in the other direction, and have been crumbling into ruin for twenty years. I purchased the entire island through one of my agents, and am rebuilding to suit my own purposes an old stone mansion which stood here before the factory was built. None notices, because my own henchmen are the workmen, and no one ever comes to this marshy island. The house is invisible from the river, hidden as it is among the tangle of old rotting warehouses. You came here in a motorboat which was anchored beneath the rotting wharves behind Shan Yang's dive. Another boat will presently fetch my men who were sent to dispose of Joan La Tour."

"They may not find that so easy," commented the detective.

"Never fear. I know she summoned that hairy wolf, Khoda Khan, to her aid, and it's true that my men failed to slay him before he reached her. But I suppose it was a false sense of trust in the Afghan that caused you to make your appointment with Kleck. I rather expected you to remain with the foolish girl and try to protect her in your way."

Somewhere below them a gong sounded. Erlik Khan did not start, but there was a surprise in the lift of his head. He closed the black book.

"I have wasted enough time on you," he said. "Once before I bade you farewell in one of my dungeons. Then the fanaticism of a crazy Druse saved you. This time there will be no upset of my plans. The only men in this house are Mongols, who know no law but my will. I go, but you will not be lonely. Soon one will come to you."

And with a low, chilling laugh the phantom-like figure moved through the door and disappeared. Outside a lock clicked, and then there was stillness.

The silence was broken suddenly by a muffled scream. It came from somewhere below and was repeated half a dozen times. Harrison shuddered. No one who has ever visited an insane asylum could fail to recognize that sound. It was the shrieking of a mad woman. After these cries the silence seemed even more stifling and menacing.

Harrison swore to quiet his feelings, and again the velvet-capped head of the Mongol leered down at him through the trap.

"Grin, you yellow-bellied ape!" roared Harrison, tugging at his cords until the veins stood out on his temples. "If I could break these damned ropes I'd knock that grin around where your pigtail ought to be, you--" He went into minute details of the Mongol's ancestry, dwelling at length on the more scandalous phases of it, and in the midst of his noisy tirade he saw the leer change suddenly to a startled snarl. The head vanished from the trap and there came a sound like the blow of a butcher's cleaver.

Then another face was poked into the trap--a wild, bearded face, with blazing, bloodshot eyes, and surmounted by a disheveled turban.

"Sahib!" hissed the apparition.

"Khoda Khan!" ejaculated the detective, galvanized. "What the devil are you doing here?"

"Softly!" muttered the Afghan. "Let not the accursed ones hear!"

He tossed the loose end of a rope ladder down through the trap and came down in a rush, his bare feet making no sound as he hit the floor. He held his long knife in his teeth, and blood dripped from the point.

Squatting beside the detective he cut him free with reckless slashes that threatened to slice flesh as well as hemp. The Afghan was quivering with half-controlled passion. His teeth gleamed like a wolf's fangs amidst the tangle of his beard.

Harrison sat up, chafing his swollen wrists.

"Where's Joan? Quick, man, where is she?"

"Here! In this accursed den!"

"But--"

"That was she screaming a few minutes ago," broke in the Afghan, and Harrison's flesh crawled with a vague monstrous premonition.

37

"But that was a mad woman!" he almost whispered.

"The sahiba is mad," said Khoda Khan somberly. "Hearken, sahib, and then judge if the fault is altogether mine.

"After you left, the accursed ones let down a man from the roof on a rope. Him I knifed, and I slew three more who sought to force the doors. But when I returned to the sahiba, she knew me not. She fled from me into the street, and other devils must have been lurking nearby, because as she ran shrieking along the sidewalk, a big automobile loomed out of the fog and a Mongol stretched forth an arm and dragged her into the car, from under my very fingers. I saw his accursed yellow face by the light of a street lamp.

"Knowing she were better dead by a bullet than in their hands, I emptied my pistol after the car, but it fled like Shaitan the Damned from the face of Allah, and if I hit anyone in it, I know not. Then as I rent my garments and cursed the day of my birth--for I could not pursue it on foot--Allah willed that another automobile should appear. It was driven by a young man in evening clothes, returning from a revel, no doubt, and being cursed with curiosity he slowed down near the curb to observe my grief.

"So, praising Allah, I sprang in beside him and placing my knife point against his ribs bade him go with speed and he obeyed in great fear. The car of the damned ones was out of sight, but presently I glimpsed it again, and exhorted the youth to greater speed, so the machine seemed to fly like the steed of the Prophet. So, presently I saw the car halt at the river bank. I made the youth halt likewise, and he sprang out and fled in the other direction in terror.

"I ran through the darkness, hot for the blood of the accursed ones, but before I could reach the bank I saw four Mongols leave the car, carrying the memsahib who was bound and gagged, and they entered a motorboat and headed out into the river toward an island which lay on the breast of the water like a dark cloud.

"I cast up and down on the shore like a madman, and was about to leap in and swim, though the distance was great, when I came upon a boat chained to a pile, but one driven by oars. I gave praise to Allah and cut the chain with my knife--see the nick in the edge?--and rowed after the accursed ones with great speed.

"They were far ahead of me, but Allah willed it that their engine should sputter and cease when they had almost reached the island. So I took heart, hearing them cursing in their heathen tongue, and hoped to draw alongside and slay them all before they were aware of me. They saw me not in the darkness, nor heard my oars because of their own noises, but before I could reach them the accursed engine began again. So they reached a wharf on the marshy shore ahead of me, but they lingered to make the boat fast, so I was not too far behind them as they bore the memsahib through the shadows of the crumbling shacks which stood all about.

"Then I was hot to overtake and slay them, but before I could come up with them they had reached the door of a great stone house--this one, sahib--set in a tangle of rotting buildings. A steel fence surrounded it, with razor-edged spearheads set along the top but by Allah, that could not hinder a lifter of the Khyber! I went over it without so much as tearing my garments. Inside was a second wall of stone, but it stood in ruins.

"I crouched in the shadows near the house and saw that the windows were heavily barred and the doors strong. Moreover, the lower part of the house is full of armed men. So I climbed a corner of the wall, and it was not easy, but presently I reached the roof which at that part is flat, with a parapet. I expected a watcher, and so there was, but he was too busy taunting his captive to see or hear me until my knife sent him to Hell. Here is his dagger; he bore no gun."

Harrison mechanically took the wicked, lean-bladed poniard.

"But what caused Joan to go mad?"

"Sahib, there was a broken wine bottle on the floor, and a goblet. I had no time to investigate it, but I know that wine must have been poisoned with the juice of the fruit called the black pomegranate. She can not have drunk much, or she would have died frothing and champing like

a mad dog. But only a little will rob one of sanity. It grows
in the jungles of Indo-China, and white men say it is a lie.
But it is no lie; thrice I have seen men die after having drunk
its juice, and more than once I have seen men, and women
too, turn mad because of it. I have traveled in that hellish
country where it grows."

"God!" Harrison's foundations were shaken by nausea.
Then his big hands clenched into chunks of iron and baleful
fire glimmered in his savage blue eyes. The weakness of
horror and revulsion was followed by cold fury dangerous as
the blood-hunger of a timber wolf.

"She may be already dead," he muttered thickly. "But
dead or alive we'll send Erlik Khan to Hell. Try that door."

It was of heavy teak, braced with bronze straps.

"It is locked," muttered the Afghan. "We will burst it."

He was about to launch his shoulder against it when he
stopped short, the long Khyber knife jumping into his fist
like a beam of light.

"Someone approaches!" he whispered, and a second
later Harrison's more civilized--and therefore duller--ears
caught a cat-like tread.

Instantly he acted. He shoved the Afghan behind
the door and sat down quickly in the center of the room,
wrapped a piece of rope about his ankles and then lay full
length, his arms behind and under him. He was lying on
the other pieces of severed cord, concealing them, and to

41

the casual glance he resembled a man lying bound hand and foot. The Afghan understood and grinned hugely.

Harrison worked with the celerity of trained mind and muscles that eliminates fumbling delay and bungling. He accomplished his purpose in a matter of seconds and without undue noise. A key grated in the lock as he settled himself, and then the door swung open. A giant Mongol stood limned in the opening. His head was shaven, his square features passionless as the face of a copper idol. In one hand he carried a curiously shaped ebony block, in the other a mace such as was borne by the horsemen of Ghengis Khan--a straight-hafted iron bludgeon with a round head covered with steel points, and a knob on the other end to keep the hand from slipping.

He did not see Khoda Khan because when he threw back the door, the Afghan was hidden behind it. Khoda Khan did not stab him as he entered because the Afghan could not see into the outer corridor, and had no way of knowing how many men were following the first. But the Mongol was alone, and he did not bother to shut the door. He went straight to the man lying on the floor, scowling slightly to see the rope ladder hanging down through the trap, as if it was not usual to leave it that way, but he did not show any suspicion or call to the man on the roof.

He did not examine Harrison's cords. The detective presented the appearance the Mongol had expected, and this fact blunted his faculties as anything taken for granted is likely to do. As he bent down, over his shoulder Harrison saw Khoda Khan glide from behind the door as silently as a panther.

Leaning his mace against his leg, spiked head on the floor, the Mongol grasped Harrison's shirt bosom with one hand, lifted his head and shoulders clear of the floor, while he shoved the block under his head. Like twin striking snakes the detective's hands whipped from behind him and locked on the Mongol's bull throat.

There was no cry; instantly the Mongol's slant eyes distended and his lips parted in a grin of strangulation. With a terrific heave he reared upright, dragging Harrison with him, but not breaking his hold, and the weight of the big American pulled them both down again. Both yellow hands tore frantically at Harrison's iron wrists; then the giant stiffened convulsively and brief agony reddened his black eyes. Khoda Khan had driven his knife between the Mongol's shoulders so that the point cut through the silk over the man's breastbone.

Harrison caught up the mace, grunting with savage satisfaction. It was a weapon more suited to his temperament than the dagger Khoda Khan had given him. No need to ask its use; if he had been bound and alone when the executioner entered, his brains would now have been clotting its spiked ball and the hollowed ebon block which so nicely accommodated a human head. Erlik Khan's executions varied along the whole gamut from the exquisitely subtle to the crudely bestial.

"The door's open," said Harrison. "Let's go!"

There were no keys on the body. Harrison doubted if the key in the door would fit any other in the building, but he locked the door and pocketed the key, hoping that would prevent the body from being soon discovered.

They emerged into a dim-lit corridor which presented the same unfinished appearance as the room they had just left. At the other end stairs wound down into shadowy gloom, and they descended warily, Harrison feeling along the wall to guide his steps. Khoda Khan seemed to see like a cat in the dark; he went down silently and surely. But it was Harrison who discovered the door. His hand, moving along the convex surface, felt the smooth stone give way to wood--a short narrow panel, through which a man could just squeeze. When the wall was covered with tapestry--as he knew it would be when Erlik Khan completed his house--it would be sufficiently hidden for a secret entrance.

Khoda Khan, behind him, was growing impatient at the delay, when somewhere below them both heard a noise simultaneously. It might have been a man ascending the winding stairs and it might not, but Harrison acted instinctively. He pushed and the door opened inward on noiseless oiled springs. A groping foot discovered narrow steps inside. With a whispered word to the Afghan he stepped through and Khoda Khan followed. He pulled the door shut again and they stood in total blackness with a curving wall on either hand. Harrison struck a match and a narrow stairs was revealed, winding down.

"This place must be built like a castle," Harrison muttered, wondering at the thickness of the walls. The match went out and they groped down in darkness too thick for even the Afghan to pierce. And suddenly both halted in their tracks. Harrison estimated that they had reached the level of the second floor, and through the inner wall came the mutter of voices. Harrison groped for another door, or a peep-hole for spying, but he found nothing of the sort. But straining his ear close to the stone, he began to understand what was being said beyond the wall, and a long-drawn hiss between clenched teeth told him that Khoda Khan likewise understood.

The first voice was Erlik Khan's; there was no mistaking that hollow reverberance. It was answered by a piteous, incoherent whimpering that brought sweat suddenly out on Harrison's flesh.

"No," the Mongol was saying. "I have come back, not from Hell as your barbarian superstitions suggest, but from a refuge unknown to your stupid police. I was saved from death by the steel cap I always wear beneath my coif. You are at a loss as to how you got here?"

"I don't understand!" It was the voice of Joan La Tour, half-hysterical, but undeniably sane. "I remember opening a bottle of wine, and as soon as I drank I knew it was drugged. Then everything faded out--I don't remember anything except great black walls, and awful shapes skulking in the darkness. I ran through gigantic shadowy halls for a thousand years--"

"They were hallucinations of madness, of the juice of the black pomegranate," answered Erlik Khan. Khoda Khan was muttering blasphemously in his beard until Harrison admonished him to silence with a fierce dig of his elbow. "If you had drunk more you would have died like a rabid dog. As it was, you went insane. But I knew the antidote-- possessed the drug that restored your sanity."

"Why?" the girl whimpered bewilderedly.

"Because I did not wish you to die like a candle blown out in the dark, my beautiful white orchid. I wish you to be fully sane so as to taste to the last dregs the shame and agony of death, subtle and prolonged. For the exquisite, an exquisite death. For the coarse-fibered, the death of an ox, such as I have decreed for your friend Harrison."

"That will be more easily decreed than executed," she retorted with a flash of spirit.

"It is already accomplished," the Mongol asserted imperturbably. "The executioner has gone to him, and by this time Mr. Harrison's head resembles a crushed egg."

"Oh, God!" At the sick grief and pain in that moan Harrison winced and fought a frantic desire to shout out denial and reassurance.

Then she remembered something else to torture her.

"Khoda Khan! What have you done with Khoda Khan?"

The Afghan's fingers clamped like iron on Harrison's arm at the sound of his name.

"When my men brought you away they did not take time to deal with him," replied the Mongol. "They had not expected to take you alive, and when fate cast you into their hands, they came away in haste. He matters little. True, he killed four of my best men, but that was merely the deed of a wolf. He has no mentality. He and the detective are much alike--mere masses of brawn, brainless, helpless against intellect like mine. Presently I shall attend to him. His corpse shall be thrown on a dung-heap with a dead pig."

"Allah!" Harrison felt Khoda Khan trembling with fury. "Liar! I will feed his yellow guts to the rats!"

Only Harrison's grip on his arm kept the maddened Moslem from attacking the stone wall in an effort to burst through to his enemy. The detective was running his hand over the surface, seeking a door, but only blank stone rewarded him. Erlik Khan had not had time to provide his unfinished house with as many secrets as his rat-runs usually possessed.

They heard the Mongol clap his hands authoritatively, and they sensed the entrance of men into the room. Staccato commands followed in Mongolian, there was a sharp cry of pain or fear, and then silence followed the soft closing of a door. Though they could not see, both men knew instinctively that the chamber on the other side of the wall was empty. Harrison almost strangled with a panic of helpless rage. He was penned in these infernal walls and Joan La Tour was being borne away to some abominable doom.

"Wallah!" the Afghan was raving. "They have taken her away to slay her! Her life and our izzat is at stake! By the Prophet's beard and my feet! I will burn this accursed house! I will slake the fire with Mongol blood! In Allah's name, sahib, let us do something!"

"Come on!" snarled Harrison. "There must be another door somewhere!"

Recklessly they plunged down the winding stair, and about the time they had reached the first floor level, Harrison's groping hand felt a door. Even as he found the catch, it moved under his fingers. Their noise must have been heard through the wall, for the panel opened, and a shaven head was poked in, framed in the square of light. The Mongol blinked in the darkness, and Harrison brought the mace down on his head, experiencing a vengeful satisfaction as he felt the skull give way beneath the iron spikes. The man fell face down in the narrow opening and Harrison sprang over his body into the outer room before he took time to learn if there were others. But the chamber was untenanted. It was thickly carpeted, the walls hung with black velvet tapestries. The doors were of bronze-bound teak, with gilt-worked arches. Khoda Khan presented an incongruous contrast, bare-footed, with draggled turban and red-smeared knife.

But Harrison did not pause to philosophize. Ignorant as he was of the house, one way was as good as another. He chose a door at random and flung it open, revealing a wide corridor carpeted and tapestried like the chamber. At the other end, through wide satin curtains that hung from roof to floor, a file of men was just disappearing--tall, black-silk clad Mongols, heads bent somberly, like a train of dusky ghosts. They did not look back.

"Follow them!" snapped Harrison. "They must be headed for the execution--"

Khoda Khan was already sweeping down the corridor like a vengeful whirlwind. The thick carpet deadened their footfalls, so even Harrison's big shoes made no noise. There was a distinct feeling of unreality, running silently down that fantastic hall--it was like a dream in which natural laws are suspended. Even in that moment Harrison had time to reflect that this whole night had been like a nightmare, possible only in the Oriental quarter, its violence and bloodshed like an evil dream. Erlik Khan had loosed the forces of chaos and insanity; murder had gone mad, and its frenzy was imparted to all actions and men caught in its maelstrom.

Khoda Khan would have burst headlong through the curtains--he was already drawing breath for a yell, and lifting his knife--if Harrison had not seized him. The Afghan's sinews were like cords under the detective's hands, and Harrison doubted his own ability to restrain him forcibly, but a vestige of sanity remained to the hillman.

Pushing him back, Harrison gazed between the curtains. There was a great double-valved door there, but it was partly open, and he looked into the room beyond. Khoda Khan's beard was jammed hard against his neck as the Afghan glared over his shoulder.

It was a large chamber, hung like the others with black velvet on which golden dragons writhed. There were thick rugs, and lanterns hanging from the ivory-inlaid ceiling cast a red glow that made for illusion. Black-robed men ranged along the wall might have been shadows but for their glittering eyes.

On a throne-like chair of ebony sat a grim figure, motionless as an image except when its loose robes stirred in the faintly moving air. Harrison felt the short hairs prickle at the back of his neck, just as a dog's hackles rise at the sight of an enemy. Khoda Khan muttered some incoherent blasphemy.

The Mongol's throne was set against a side wall. No one stood near him as he sat in solitary magnificence, like an idol brooding on human doom. In the center of the room stood what looked uncomfortably like a sacrificial altar--a curiously carved block of stone that might have come out of the heart of the Gobi. On that stone lay Joan La Tour, white as a marble statue, her arms outstretched like a crucifix, her hands and feet extending over the edges of the block. Her dilated eyes stared upward as one lost to hope, aware of doom and eager only for death to put an end to agony. The physical torture had not yet begun, but a gaunt half-naked brute squatted on his haunches at the end of the altar, heating the point of a bronze rod in a dish full of glowing coals.

"Damn!" It was half curse, half sob of fury bursting from Harrison's lips. Then he was hurled aside and Khoda Khan burst into the room like a flying dervish, bristling beard, blazing eyes, knife and all. Erlik Khan came erect with a startled guttural as the Afghan came tearing down the room like a headlong hurricane of destruction. The torturer sprang up just in time to meet the yard-long knife lashing down, and it split his skull down through the teeth.

"Aie!" It was a howl from a score of Mongol throats.

"Allaho akabar!" yelled Khoda Khan, whirling the red knife about his head. He threw himself on the altar, slashing at Joan's bonds with a frenzy that threatened to dismember the girl.

Then from all sides the black-robed figures swarmed in, not noticing in their confusion that the Afghan had been followed by another grim figure who came with less abandon but with equal ferocity.

They were aware of Harrison only when he dealt a prodigious sweep of his mace, right and left, bowling men over like ten-pins, and reached the altar through the gap made in the bewildered throng. Khoda Khan had freed the girl and he wheeled, spitting like a cat, his bared teeth gleaming and each hair of his beard stiffly on end.

"Allah!" he yelled--spat in the faces of the oncoming Mongols--crouched as if to spring into the midst of them-- then whirled and rushed headlong at the ebony throne.

The speed and unexpectedness of the move were stunning. With a choked cry Erlik Khan fired and missed at point-blank range--and then the breath burst from Khoda Khan in an ear-splitting yell as his knife plunged into the Mongol's breast and the point sprang a hand's breadth out of his black-clad back.

The impetus of his rush unchecked, Khoda Khan hurtled into the falling figure, crashing it back onto the ebony throne which splintered under the impact of the two heavy bodies. Bounding up, wrenching his dripping knife free, Khoda Khan whirled it high and howled like a wolf.

"Ya Allah! Wearer of steel caps! Carry the taste of my knife in your guts to Hell with you!"

There was a long hissing intake of breath as the Mongols stared wide-eyed at the black-robed, red-smeared figure crumpled grotesquely among the ruins of the broken throne; and in the instant that they stood like frozen men, Harrison caught up Joan and ran for the nearest door, bellowing: "Khoda Khan! This way! Quick!"

With a howl and a whickering of blades the Mongols were at his heels. Fear of steel in his back winged Harrison's big feet, and Khoda Khan ran slantingly across the room to meet him at the door.

"Haste, sahib! Down the corridor! I will cover you retreat!"

"No! Take Joan and run!" Harrison literally threw her into the Afghan's arms and wheeled back in the doorway, lifting the mace. He was as berserk in his own way as was Khoda Khan, frantic with the madness that sometimes inspired men in the midst of combat.

The Mongols came on as if they, too, were blood-mad. They jammed the door with square snarling faces and squat silk-clad bodies before he could slam it shut. Knives licked at him, and gripping the mace with both hands he wielded it like a flail, working awful havoc among the shapes that strove in the doorway, wedged by the pressure from behind. The lights, the upturned snarling faces that dissolved in crimson ruin beneath his flailing, all swam in a red mist. He was not aware of his individual identity. He was only a man with a club, transported back fifty thousand years, a hairy-breasted, red-eyed primitive, wholly possessed in the crimson instinct for slaughter.

He felt like howling his incoherent exultation with each swing of his bludgeon that crushed skulls and spattered blood into his face. He did not feel the knives that found him, hardly realizing it when the men facing him gave back, daunted at the havoc he was wreaking. He did not close the door then; it was blocked and choked by a ghastly mass of crushed and red-dripping flesh.

He found himself running down the corridor, his breath coming in great gulping gasps, following some dim instinct of preservation or realization of duty that made itself heard amidst the red dizzy urge to grip his foes and strike, strike, strike, until he was himself engulfed in the crimson waves of death. In such moments the passion to die--die fighting--is almost equal to the will to live.

In a daze, staggering, bumping into walls and caroming off them, he reached the further end of the corridor where Khoda Khan was struggling with a lock. Joan was standing now, though she reeled on her feet, and seemed on the point of collapse. The mob was coming down the long corridor full cry behind them. Drunkenly Harrison thrust Khoda Khan aside and whirling the blood-fouled mace around his head, struck a stupendous blow that shattered the lock, burst the bolts out of their sockets and caved in the heavy panels as if they had been cardboard. The next instant they were through and Khoda Khan slammed the ruins of the door which sagged on its hinges, but somehow held together. There were heavy metal brackets on each jamb, and Khoda Khan found and dropped an iron bar in place just as the mob surged against it.

Through the shattered panels they howled and thrust their knives, but Harrison knew until they hewed away enough wood to enable them to reach in and dislodge it, the bar across the door would hold the splintered barrier in place. Recovering some of his wits, and feeling rather sick, he herded his companions ahead of him with desperate haste. He noticed, briefly, that he was stabbed in the calf, thigh, arm and shoulder. Blood soaked his ribboned shirt and ran down his limbs in streams. The Mongols were hacking at the door, snarling like jackals over carrion.

The apertures were widening, and through then he saw other Mongols running down the corridor with rifles; just as he wondered why they did not shoot through the door, then saw the reason. They were in a chamber which had been converted into a magazine. Cartridge cases were piled high along the wall, and there was at least one box of dynamite. But he looked in vain for rifles or pistols. Evidently they were stored in another part of the building.

Khoda Khan was jerking bolts on an opposite door, but he paused to glare about and yelping "Allah!" he pounced on an open case, snatched something out--wheeled, yelled a curse and threw back his arm, but Harrison grabbed his wrist.

"Don't throw that, you idiot! You'll blow us all to Hell! They're afraid to shoot into this room, but they'll have that door down in a second or so, and finish us with their knives. Help Joan!"

It was a hand grenade Khoda Khan had found--the only one in an otherwise empty case, as a glance assured Harrison. The detective threw the door open, slammed it shut behind them as they plunged out into the starlight, Joan reeling, half carried by the Afghan. They seemed to have emerged at the back of the house. They ran across an open space, hunted creatures looking for a refuge. There was a crumbling stone wall, about breast-high to a man, and they ran through a wide gap in it, only to halt, a groan bursting from Harrison's lips. Thirty steps behind the ruined wall rose the steel fence of which Khoda Khan had spoken, a barrier ten feet high, topped with keen points. The door crashed open behind them and a gun spat venomously. They were in a trap. If they tried to climb the fence the Mongols had but to pick them off like monkeys shot off a ladder.

"Down behind the wall!" snarled Harrison, forcing Joan behind an uncrumbled section of the stone barrier. "We'll make 'em pay for it, before they take us!"

The door was crowded with snarling faces, now leering in triumph. There were rifles in the hands of a dozen. They knew their victims had no firearms, and could not escape, and they themselves could use rifles without fear. Bullets began to splatter on the stone, then with a long-drawn yell Khoda Khan bounded to the top of the wall, ripping out the pin of the hand grenade with his teeth.

"La illaha illulah; Muhammad rassoul ullah!" he yelled, and hurled the bomb--not at the group which howled and ducked, but over their heads, into the magazine!

The next instant a rending crash tore the guts out of the night and a blinding blaze of fire ripped the darkness apart. In that glare Harrison had a glimpse of Khoda Khan, etched against the flame, hurtling backward, arms out-thrown--then there was utter blackness in which roared the thunder of the fall of the house of Erlik Khan as the shattered walls buckled, the beams splintered, the roof fell in and story after story came crashing down on the crumpled foundations.

How long Harrison lay like dead he never knew, blinded, deafened and paralyzed; covered by falling debris. His first realization was that there was something soft under him, something that writhed and whimpered. He had a vague feeling he ought not to hurt this soft something, so he began to shove the broken stones and mortar off him. His arm seemed dead, but eventually he excavated himself and staggered up, looking like a scarecrow in his rags. He groped among the rubble, grasped the girl and pulled her up.

"Joan!" His own voice seemed to come to him from a great distance; he had to shout to make her hear him. Their eardrums had been almost split by the concussion.

"Are you hurt?" He ran his one good hand over her to make sure.

"I don't think so," she faltered dazedly. "What--what happened?"

"Khoda Khan's bomb exploded the dynamite. The house fell in on the Mongols. We were sheltered by that wall; that's all that saved us."

The wall was a shattered heap of broken stone, half covered by rubble--a waste of shattered masonry with broken beams thrust up through the litter, and shards of walls reeling drunkenly. Harrison fingered his broken arm and tried to think, his head swimming.

"Where is Khoda Khan?" cried Joan, seeming finally to shake off her daze.

"I'll look for him." Harrison dreaded what he expected to find. "He was blown off the wall like a straw in a wind."

Stumbling over broken stones and bits of timber, he found the Afghan huddled grotesquely against the steel fence. His fumbling fingers told him of broken bones--but

58

the man was still breathing. Joan came stumbling toward him, to fall beside Khoda Khan and flutter her quick fingers over him, sobbing hysterically.

"He's not like civilized man!" she exclaimed, tears running down her stained, scratched face. "Afghans are harder than cats to kill. If we could get him medical attention he'll live. Listen!" She caught Harrison's arm with galvanized fingers; but he had heard it too--the sputter of a motor that was probably a police launch, coming to investigate the explosion.

Joan was tearing her scanty garments to pieces to staunch the blood that seeped from the Afghan's wounds, when miraculously Khoda Khan's pulped lips moved. Harrison, bending close, caught fragments of words: "The curse of Allah--Chinese dog--swine's flesh--my izzat."

"You needn't worry about your izzat," grunted Harrison, glancing at the ruins which hid the mangled figures that had been Mongolian terrorists. "After this night's work you'll not go to jail--not for all the Chinamen in River Street."

THE END